At the Dance Class

Written by Roderick Hunt and Annemarie Young

Illustrated by Nick Schon,
based on the original characters
created by Alex Brychta

Sam and his dad came to see Kipper. Sam had something to ask.

"I want to have ballet lessons," he said. "Will you come too?"

"Sam wants to be a footballer," said his dad. "And ballet will help. It's really good for developing strength and football moves."

Kipper wasn't sure he'd like going to dance classes.

"Please come. We'll have fun," said Sam.

In the end, Kipper agreed to have a go. He was glad to see one of his other friends was there too. Anna waved and came over.

The ballet class was fun. Mary, the teacher, made them do funny walks. Then they had to stop suddenly. It was hard not to fall over.

The children liked Mary's helper, Leo. When Mary asked everyone to make a scary shape with their arms, Leo made them all laugh.

A week later, Mary told the children to get into groups. “Think of an insect,” she told them. “Then try to move just like that insect.”

Kipper, Sam and Anna decided to be crickets. “We can crouch down and jump up suddenly,” said Sam.

Jumping like a cricket was hard.

Leo showed the children
how to bend down
and then
jump up.

“Now we’ll add some music,” said Mary. “Try to move in time to the music.”

At the next lesson they learned how to skip. “Hop on one leg, then step with the other,” said Mary. “That’s right, Kipper. Well done.”

Sam and Anna watched Kipper.
Then they hopped and stepped.
Soon they were all skipping.
"This is fun!" said Kipper.

The following week, Mary said, "You're very good at being insects, so we're going to do The Bugs Ballet for the end of term show."

Sam and Anna were excited.
Kipper wasn't sure. Then Leo said,
"I'm going to dance too. I'm a wasp!"
"That'll be fun," said Kipper.

Mum and Anna's dad were making the cricket costumes. The children were practising being crickets. It was hard.